ADAM SANDLER

ACTOR & COMEDIAN

KATIE LAJINESS

Big Buddy Books
An Imprint of Abdo Publishing
abdopublishing.com

BIG BUDDY POP BIOGRAPHIES

abdopublishing.com

Published by Abdo Publishing, a division of ABDO, PO Box 398166, Minneapolis, Minnesota 55439.
Copyright © 2016 by Abdo Consulting Group, Inc. International copyrights reserved in all countries. No part of this book may be reproduced in any form without written permission from the publisher. Big Buddy Books™ is a trademark and logo of Abdo Publishing.

Printed in the United States of America, North Mankato, Minnesota.
102015
012016

Cover Photo: © LAN/Corbis.
Interior Photos: © AF archive/Alamy (pp. 13, 17); Associated Press (pp. 9, 13, 15, 17, 29); James DeVaney/Getty Images (p. 23); Fotos International/Getty Images (p. 5); Getty Images (p. 25); Tim Mosenfelder/Getty Images (pp. 19, 27); New York Daily News Archive/Getty Images (p. 9); Chris Pizzello/Invision/AP/AP Photo (p. 21); Alberto E. Rodriguez/Getty Images (p. 6); Matt Sayles/InvisionAP/AP Photo (p. 31); Universal Pictures/Getty Images (p. 11).

Coordinating Series Editor: Tamara L. Britton
Contributing Editor: Marcia Zappa
Graphic Design: Jenny Christensen

Library of Congress Cataloging-in-Publication Data

Lajiness, Katie.
Adam Sandler / Katie Lajiness.
pages cm. -- (Big buddy pop biographies)
Includes index.
ISBN 978-1-68078-059-8
1. Sandler, Adam--Juvenile literature. 2. Actors--United States--Biography--Juvenile literature. 3. Comedians--United States--Biography--Juvenile literature. I. Title.
PN2287.S275L35 2016
791.4302'8092--dc23
[B]

2015028984

CONTENTS

TOTALLY TALENTED

Adam Sandler is a talented and popular **entertainer**. He is an actor, writer, singer, and **producer**. Adam is best known for starring in funny movies.

DID YOU KNOW?
Adam has acted in more than 50 movies and television shows!

SNAPSHOT

NAME:
Adam Richard Sandler

BIRTHDAY:
September 9, 1966

BIRTHPLACE:
New York City, New York

POPULAR MOVIES:
Billy Madison, *Happy Gilmore*, *The Waterboy*, *Big Daddy*, and *Hotel Transylvania*

FAMILY TIES

Adam Richard Sandler was born in New York City, New York, on September 9, 1966. He was raised in Manchester, New Hampshire. His parents are Stanley and Judy Sandler. Adam has two sisters and one brother. His family is **Jewish**.

Growing up, Adam's mother (*right*) taught young children. His father created electronics.

WHERE IN THE WORLD?

CANADA
Maine
Vermont
New Hampshire
Manchester
New York
Massachusetts
Rhode Island
Connecticut
Pennsylvania
New York City
ATLANTIC OCEAN
New Jersey
N
W
E
S

STARTING OUT

At age 17, Adam **performed** his first **stand-up comedy** act. Before long, he started to get parts in television shows.

Adam's first **role** was on *The Cosby Show* in 1987. He was part of MTV's game show *Remote Control*. From 1990 to 1995, Adam was a writer and actor on *Saturday Night Live*.

In 1987, Adam performed his comedy act at Comic Strip Live in New York City.

In school, Adam was the class clown.

RISING STAR

Adam's first big movie was *Billy Madison* in 1995. In it, he plays a man who has to repeat all 12 grades. If Billy **graduates** from high school, then he can run his father's company.

Fans loved *Billy Madison*. But some movie critics did not enjoy the movie. Adam did not let their bad reviews stop him from making movies.

DID YOU KNOW

Adam wrote *Billy Madison* with Tim Herlihy. Adam and Tim worked together on *Saturday Night Live*. They went on to make many movies together.

Billy Madison earned more than $25 million at the box office.

MOVIE MAKER

Adam continued to make **entertaining** movies. He had many hits in the 1990s. These included *Happy Gilmore*, *The Wedding Singer*, *The Waterboy*, and *Big Daddy*.

Adam's movies made a lot of money at the box office. *Big Daddy* made more than $160 million!

Actress Drew Barrymore appeared in three movies with Adam. These include *The Wedding Singer* (above), *50 First Dates*, and *Blended* (right).

MOVIES WITH FRIENDS

Many of Adam's friends are also famous actors. He often asks them to appear in his movies. They include Chris Rock, Kevin James, Nick Swardson, and Steve Buscemi. Rob Schneider has been in about 20 movies with Adam!

In 2010, Adam worked with friends Chris Rock (*left*), Kevin James (*second from right*), and Rob Schneider (*right*) on the movie *Grown Ups*.

NEW OPPORTUNITIES

Adam also works on television and in cartoons. In 2014, he was in an **episode** of *Brooklyn Nine-Nine* with his friend Andy Samberg.

In 2012, Adam was the voice of Dracula in *Hotel Transylvania*. The movie was so popular that Adam made *Hotel Transylvania 2* in 2015.

In *Hotel Transylvania,* Dracula runs a hotel for monsters.

Adam, Selena Gomez, and Kevin James *(left to right)* worked together on *Hotel Transylvania*.

SILLY SONGS

Adam is known for writing and singing funny songs. He often **performed** them on *Saturday Night Live*. And, he recorded them on albums. "Lunch Lady Land" and "The Thanksgiving Song" were two of Adam's most popular songs.

In 1999, "The Chanukah Song" spent two weeks on Billboard's Hot 100 list.

WINNING BIG

Adam goes to a lot of **award** shows. He has won many awards. He has Kids' Choice Awards, MTV Movie Awards, and People's Choice Awards in his collection.

DID YOU KNOW?

Adam has also won many Razzie Awards. These silly awards honor the worst actors, actresses, and films of the year.

In 2015, Adam won the Favorite Comedic Movie Actor award at the People's Choice Awards.

BEHIND THE CAMERA

In 1999, Adam started Happy Madison **Productions**. The company's name combines two of his most famous movies, *Happy Gilmore* and *Billy Madison*.

Adam's company produces his movies as well as movies starring other actors. It produced *Paul Blart: Mall Cop* starring his friend Kevin James.

In 2008, Happy Madison Productions made *You Don't Mess with the Zohan*. Production companies do a lot of work behind the scenes of a movie.

OFF THE SCREEN

On June 22, 2003, Adam married actress Jackie Titone. Jackie has appeared in movies such as *Bedtime Stories*.

Adam and Jackie have two daughters. Sadie was born in 2006. And, Sunny was born in 2008.

Adam and Jackie were married in Malibu, California.

A HELPING HAND

Adam enjoys helping people. In 2007, he gave $1 million to the Boys and Girls Club in Manchester.

Adam has also worked with Toys for Tots. He helped needy children receive new toys during the holidays.

DID YOU KNOW?
Adam worked with the Make-A-Wish Foundation. He asked an ill boy to be an extra in one of his movies!

Adam often supports causes by performing. In 2015, he and Train singer Pat Monahan (*left*) sang to raise money for sick children.

BUZZ

Adam was very busy making movies in 2015. That summer, *Pixels* came out. In it, Adam plays Sam Brenner. He fights video game characters from outer space.

Adam also **produced** and starred in the movie *The Ridiculous 6* for Netflix. It came out in winter of 2015. Fans are excited for what Adam Sandler will do next!

Fans enjoyed seeing Adam slime Josh Gad at the 2015 Kids' Choice Awards.

GLOSSARY

award something that is given in recognition of good work or a good act.

entertain amusement or pleasure that comes from watching a performer. An entertainer is one who provides entertainment.

episode one show in a series of shows.

graduate (GRA-juh-wayt) to complete a level of schooling.

Jewish of or related to a person who practices Judaism, which is a religion based on laws recorded in the Torah, or is related to the ancient Hebrews.

perform to do something in front of an audience.

produce to oversee the making of a movie, a play, an album, or a radio or television show. A person who does this is called a producer. The finished work is known as a production.

role a part an actor plays.

stand-up comedy jokes and funny stories told to a crowd by a performer.

WEBSITES

To learn more about Pop Biographies, visit **booklinks.abdopublishing.com**. These links are routinely monitored and updated to provide the most current information available.

INDEX